FASCINATING FACTS

U.S. PRESIDENTS

BY SHERYL PETERSON

Published by The Child's World®
1980 Lookout Drive • Mankato, MN 56003-1705
800-599-READ • www.childsworld.com

Photographs ©: Shutterstock Images, cover (baseball), cover (saxophone), cover (raccoon), cover (broccoli), cover (Chester A. Arthur), cover (White House), 1 (baseball), 1 (saxophone), 1 (raccoon), 1 (broccoli), 1 (Chester A. Arthur), 1 (White House), 2, 3, 4, 7, 8, 8–9, 10, 11, 12, 13, 14, 14–15, 16–17 (snake), 16–17 (tadpole), 18, 19, 21, 24, back cover (teddy bear), back cover (ice cream); Ron Edmonds/AP Images, 5; Doug Mills/AP Images, 6, 17; Chris O'Meara/AP Images, 20–21

Copyright © 2021 by The Child's World®
All rights reserved. No part of this book may be reproduced or utilized in any form or by any means without written permission from the publisher.

ISBN 9781503844599 (Reinforced Library Binding)
ISBN 9781503846326 (Portable Document Format)
ISBN 9781503847514 (Online Multi-user eBook)
LCCN 2019957941

Printed in the United States of America

ABOUT THE AUTHOR

Sheryl Peterson is the author of many nonfiction books for young readers. She lives near the Canadian border in International Falls, MN.

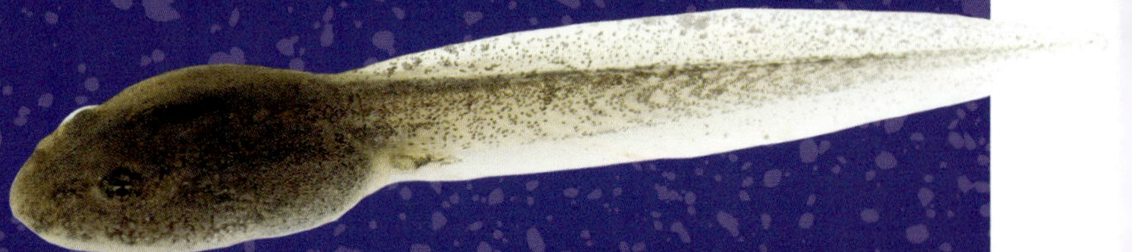

CONTENTS

Introduction . . . 4

CHAPTER ONE
Presidents Play . . . 6

CHAPTER TWO
Life in the White House . . . 10

CHAPTER THREE
First Families . . . 14

CHAPTER FOUR
Strange but True Tales . . . 18

Glossary . . . 22

To Learn More . . . 23

Index . . . 24

INTRODUCTION

U.S. presidents have an important job. They make hard decisions for the American people. They meet with leaders in other countries to keep peace.

Presidents and their families have daily lives like everybody else. They have pets, nicknames, and favorite foods. Some like to exercise or play games. Others read or practice musical instruments in their free time.

Enjoy learning some cool and crazy facts about many of the presidents and their families!

CHAPTER ONE

Presidents Play

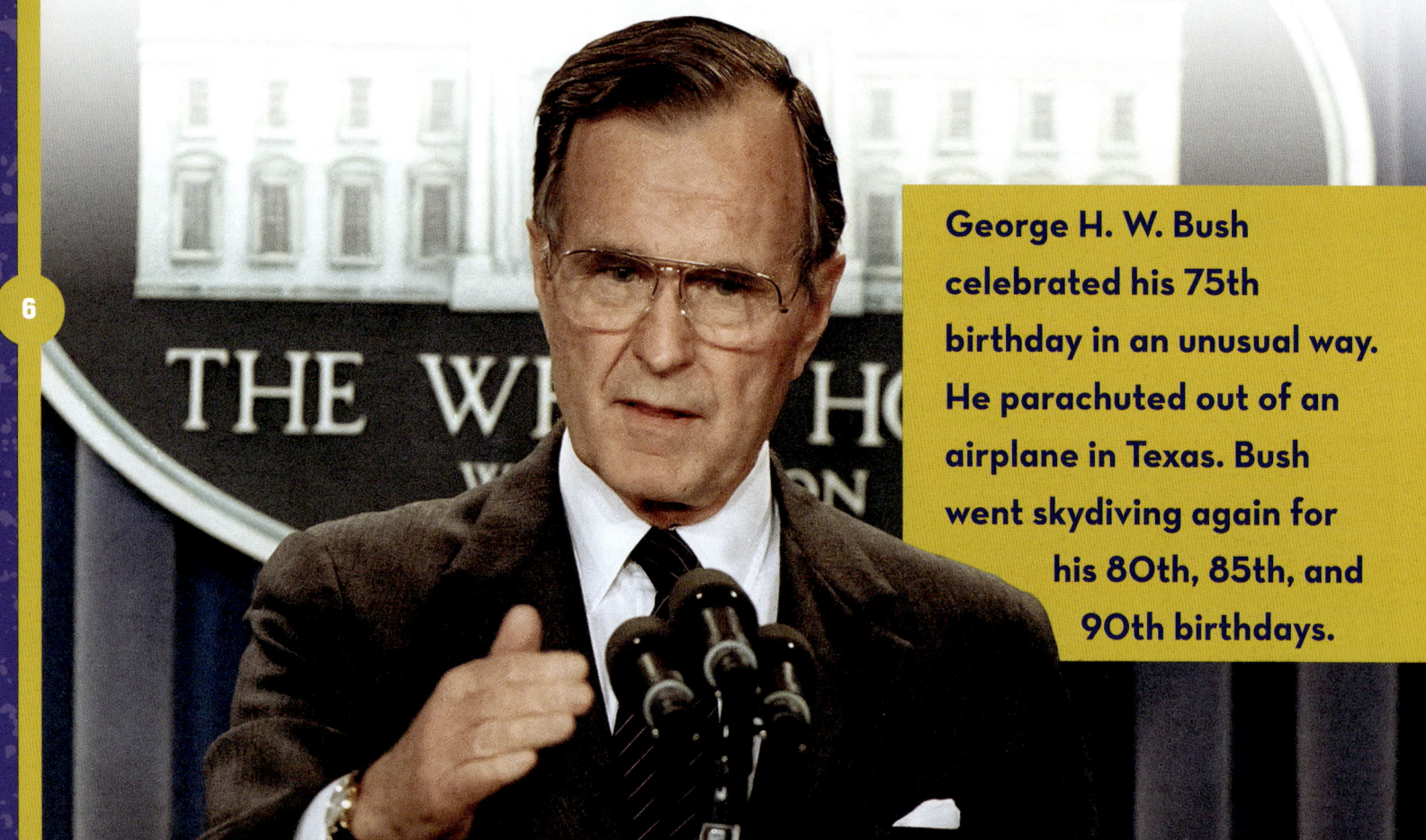

George H. W. Bush celebrated his 75th birthday in an unusual way. He parachuted out of an airplane in Texas. Bush went skydiving again for his 80th, 85th, and 90th birthdays.

In 1910, William Taft was the first president to pitch a ball to start the baseball season. He stood up in his seat and tossed the ball to the pitcher. As of 2019, Donald Trump is the first president since Taft who has not thrown the opening pitch of a major league game. ▲

George W. Bush, Ronald Reagan, Dwight D. Eisenhower, and Franklin D. Roosevelt were all cheerleaders while in college.

size 14

▲ Warren Harding was a golfer with the biggest feet of any president. His golf shoes were size 14! Those shoes, as well as his slippers, are on display at the Smithsonian Museum in Washington, DC.

Presidential Pastimes

Theodore "Teddy" Roosevelt was an outdoorsman and hunter. However, on one hunting trip he refused to shoot a bear. A toymaker named a stuffed animal after him called the Teddy Bear! ▶

Theodore Roosevelt had a **photographic memory**. He could repeat an entire newspaper page he had read. It was as if he was reading right from the paper!

Calvin Coolidge liked to ride horses—until the Secret Service said it was too dangerous. Instead, he got an electric horse, a machine that mimicked the sensation of riding a real horse. He named it Thunderbolt. It was shaped like a barrel with a neck of wood, metal, and leather.

◀ When he was a child, Richard Nixon's mother made him practice on an instrument every afternoon. He learned to play the piano, violin, accordion, saxophone, and clarinet.

◀ Bill Clinton played the saxophone in a jazz trio called "The Three Kings." The group was nicknamed "The Three Blind Mice," because the players wore dark sunglasses. Clinton continued to play saxophone while president.

CHAPTER TWO

Life in the White House

Franklin D. Roosevelt's dog was named Fala. Every day, Fala was served a bone on the president's breakfast tray. The dog was so popular, he was given his own secretary to answer his fan mail. A statue of Fala is in the Franklin D. Roosevelt Memorial in Washington, DC.
▼

Abraham Lincoln's son Tad had two pet goats named Nanny and Nanko. He liked to harness up his goats to a sled. One time, the goats pulled Tad right through the middle of a White House party.

James Buchanan was given a herd of elephants by the king of Siam (now Thailand). He gave the elephants to a zoo.

Lyndon B. Johnson had two beagles named Him and Her. Him fathered puppies. Johnson's daughter Luci kept two. She named the puppies Kim and Freckles.

Calvin Coolidge had two pet raccoons named Rueben and Rebecca. Ruben escaped the White House, but Rebecca had her own little house on the White House lawn. ▼

Everyday Life

George H. W. Bush did not like broccoli. As president, he made a rule that it could not be served to him in the White House! ▼

Franklin D. Roosevelt was **superstitious** about the number 13. He refused to have 13 people at his dinner table. He would never leave for an important trip on Friday the 13th.

Herbert Hoover wanted his White House servants to be almost invisible. When he entered a room, the servants had to jump quickly into a closet and hide. If they didn't, they would be fired.

Chester A. Arthur loved clothes. He owned about 80 pairs each of pants and shoes. Arthur changed clothes many times a day and always wore a tuxedo to dinner. He didn't have a bodyguard, but he did have a servant to take care of his clothes.

80
PAIRS OF PANTS AND SHOES

CHAPTER THREE
First Families

Hillary Clinton often ate a hot pepper or sprinkled hot sauce on her food. She said it kept her **immune system** healthy. She continues to keep hot sauce in her purse, so she always has it.

Mary Todd Lincoln was only 5 feet, 2 inches (1.55 m) tall. Her husband, Abraham Lincoln, was 6 feet, 4 inches (1.9 m). They loved to dance together, but the pair looked a little odd.

Betty Ford was a popular First Lady. When Gerald Ford was running for reelection, buttons were made that said, "Elect Betty's husband. Keep Betty in the White House!"

Julia Tyler would have a band play the song "Hail to the Chief" when John Tyler entered a party after he became president in 1841. Bands still play the song when the president arrives somewhere.

Mamie Eisenhower spent one day a week in bed while First Lady. A skin specialist said she would never get wrinkles if she did that. The White House maids called her "Sleeping Beauty."

◀ Dolley Madison loved ice cream. In the 1800s, it was a rare treat because freezers had not yet been invented. She even served oyster ice cream!

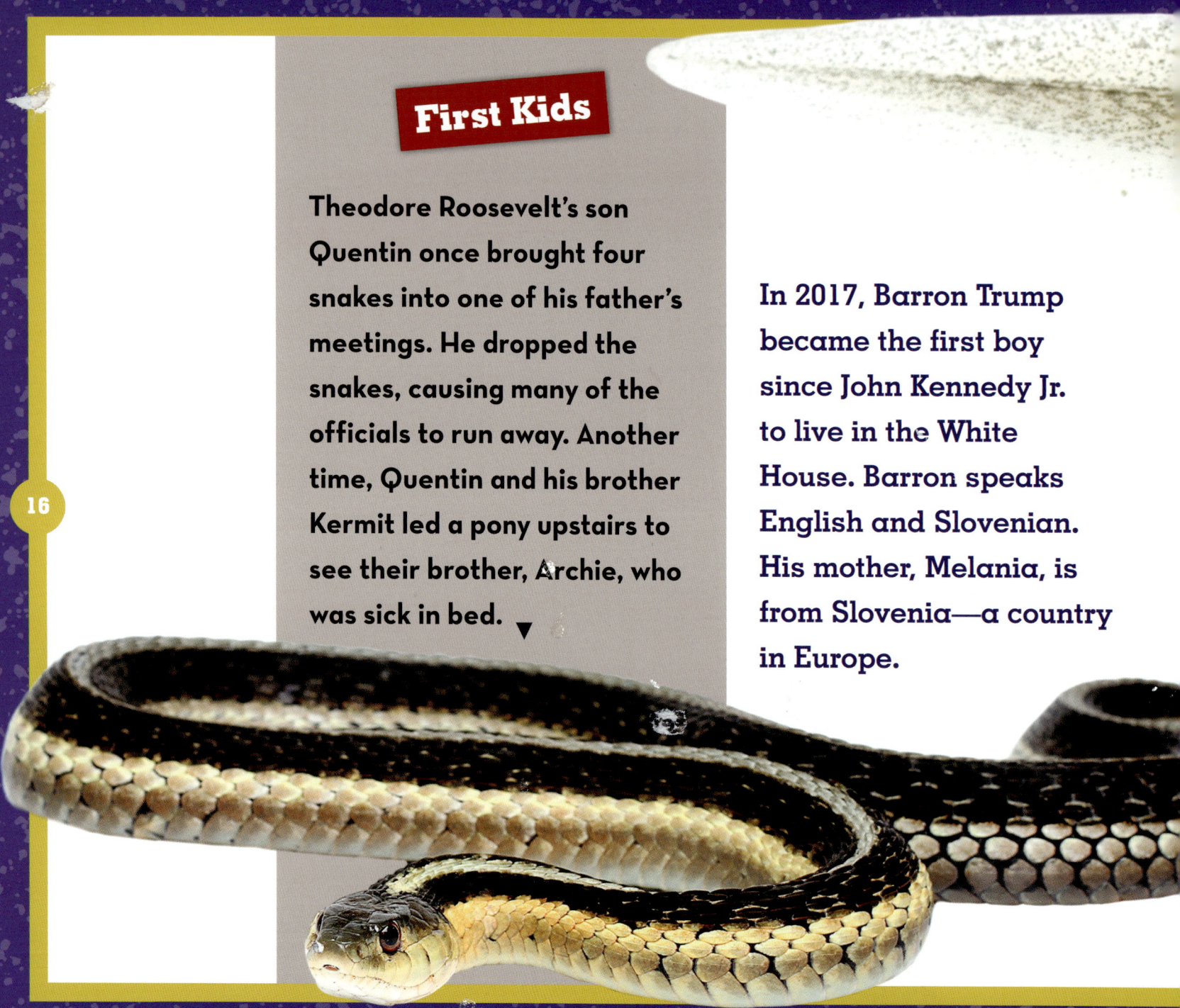

First Kids

Theodore Roosevelt's son Quentin once brought four snakes into one of his father's meetings. He dropped the snakes, causing many of the officials to run away. Another time, Quentin and his brother Kermit led a pony upstairs to see their brother, Archie, who was sick in bed. ▼

In 2017, Barron Trump became the first boy since John Kennedy Jr. to live in the White House. Barron speaks English and Slovenian. His mother, Melania, is from Slovenia—a country in Europe.

▲ Abraham Lincoln's son Tad was really named Thomas. His father nicknamed him Tad because he looked like a tadpole as a baby.

As of 2019, George W. Bush's daughters Barbara and Jenna were the first and only twins to live in the White House. ▶

CHAPTER FOUR

Strange but True Tales

Grover Cleveland is counted as both the 22nd and 24th president. As of 2019, he is the only president to have served two **nonconsecutive** terms.

Martin Van Buren, the eighth president, was the first to be born as a U.S. citizen. The first seven presidents were born before the Declaration of Independence was written. This means they were originally British citizens.

Benjamin Harrison was the first president to have electric lights. However, he and his wife Anna would not touch the light switches. They were so afraid of getting shocks that they made staff members turn the lights on and off for them.

George Washington may have been the first president, but he was not the first to live in the White House. Washington helped choose the design of the White House, but his **successor**, John Adams, was the first president to live there.

Odd Stories

Lyndon B. Johnson liked to trick guests at his Texas ranch. He would take them in his blue convertible to the top of a hill and pretend the brakes didn't work. The car would zoom into a lake. Johnson would laugh because his car was an "amphicar" that turned into a speedboat!

George Washington lost most of his teeth. New teeth were made from animal teeth, **ivory**, and different metals. When Washington was president, he only had one real tooth left in his mouth.

Barack Obama's first job was working for an ice cream store. He ate too much ice cream at the job and is still not a fan of the sweet treat today.

Calvin Coolidge once woke up in a hotel room and found a burglar. Coolidge calmly talked to the man and found out he needed money for his hotel room and a train ticket back to his college. The president loaned him money, which the man paid back. ▶

John Adams and Thomas Jefferson never agreed on politics, but both died on the same day. It was July 4, 1826—the 50th anniversary of the Declaration of Independence. James Monroe died on the same day five years later.

3 miles

◀ John F. Kennedy was an officer in the navy during World War II (1939–1945). When his boat was hit and sunk, he and his men swam more than 3 miles (4.8 km) to safety. He carved a message asking for help onto a coconut. Two men from the Solomon Islands found the crew and brought the coconut to Allied troops, who rescued Kennedy and his men. Later, as president, he kept the coconut in the **Oval Office**.

Glossary

immune system (im-MYOON SIS-tum) The immune system protects the body from germs and bacteria. Eating fruits and vegetables help strengthen the immune system.

ivory (EYE-vor-ee) Ivory is the hard white part of an animal's tusk. Elephant tusks are made of ivory.

nonconsecutive (non-kun-SEK-yoo-tiv) Something that is nonconsecutive happens multiple times, but not in a row. Only one president has served nonconsecutive terms.

Oval Office (OH-vul OFF-iss) The Oval Office is the president's main working spot in the White House. The president gave a speech in the Oval Office.

photographic memory (foh-toh-GRAF-ik MEM-uh-ree) A photographic memory is the ability to remember a large amount of information at once. Theodore Roosevelt had a photographic memory.

successor (suk-SESS-ur) A successor is the person who has a position after another person. Donald Trump was Barack Obama's successor.

superstitious (SOO-per-STISH-uss) People are superstitious when they believe in magic, fate, or luck. Some people are superstitious about black cats crossing their paths.

trio (TREE-oh) A trio is a group of three things or performers. Bill Clinton played saxophone in a trio.

To Learn More

In the Library

DuMont, Brianna. *U.S. Presidents.*
Washington, DC: National Geographic, 2017.

Flynn, Sarah. *1,000 Facts about the White House.*
Washington, DC: National Geographic, 2017.

Parker, Philip. *The Presidents Visual Encyclopedia.*
New York, NY: DK Publishing, 2017.

On the Web

Visit our website for links about the U.S. Presidents:
childsworld.com/links

Note to Parents, Teachers, and Librarians: We routinely verify our Web links to make sure they are safe and active sites. So encourage your readers to check them out!

Index

Adams, John, 19, 21
Arthur, Chester A., 13

Buchanan, James, 11
Bush, George H. W., 6, 12
Bush, George W., 7, 17

Cleveland, Grover, 18
Clinton, Bill, 9
Coolidge, Calvin, 9, 11, 21

Eisenhower, Dwight D., 7

Harding, Warren, 7
Harrison, Benjamin, 18
Hoover, Herbert, 12

Jefferson, Thomas, 21
Johnson, Lyndon B., 11, 20

Kennedy, John F., 21

Lincoln, Abraham, 11, 14, 17

Monroe, James, 21

Nixon, Richard, 9

Obama, Barack, 20

Reagan, Ronald, 7
Roosevelt, Franklin D., 7, 10, 12
Roosevelt, Theodore "Teddy," 8, 16

Taft, William, 7
Trump, Donald, 7

Van Buren, Martin, 18

Washington, George, 19, 20